Ladybird Readers

Doctor Panda

Notes to teachers, parents, and carers

The *Ladybird Readers* Starter level gently introduces children to the phonics approach to reading, by covering familiar themes that young readers will have studied (for example, colors, animals, and family).

Phonics focuses on how the individual sounds of letters are blended together to sound out a word. For example, /c/ /a/ /t/ when put together sound out the word **cat**.

The Starter level is divided into two sub-level sections:
• **A** looks at simple words, such as **ant**, **dog**, and **red**.
• **B** explores trickier sound–letter combinations, such as the **/igh/** sound in **night** and **fright**.

This book looks at the theme of **parts of the body** and focuses on these sounds and letters:

h   ee   oo (long)   oo (short)

There are some activities to do in this book. They will help children practice these skills:

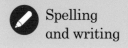 Spelling and writing   Speaking   Reading

LADYBIRD BOOKS
UK | USA | Canada | Ireland | Australia
India | New Zealand | South Africa
Ladybird Books is part of the Penguin Random House group of companies
whose addresses can be found at global.penguinrandomhouse.com.
www.penguin.co.uk   www.puffin.co.uk   www.ladybird.co.uk

Penguin
Random House
UK

First published 2017
001

Copyright © Ladybird Books Ltd, 2017
The moral rights of the author and illustrator have been asserted.

Printed in China

A CIP catalogue record for this book is available from the British Library

ISBN: 978–0–241–28339–4

All correspondence to Ladybird Books
Penguin Random House Childrens
80 Strand, London WC2R 0RL

Doctor Panda

Look at the story

Series Editor: Sorrel Pitts
Story by Coleen Degnan-Veness
Illustrated by Chris Jevons

Picture words

Andy Ant

Doctor Panda

Dom Dog

Gus Goat

Pat Cat

head

look

Aa Bb Cc Dd Ee Ff Gg Hh Ii Jj Kk Ll Mi

Letters and sounds: **h ee oo** (long) **oo** (short)
Theme: **parts of the body**

bag

book

eyes

feet

garden

hand

hot

mouth

sit

Use these words to help you with the activity on page 16.

Dom Dog

Pat Cat

garden

hot

7

head   **hand**   **mouth**

9

Doctor Panda

bag

eyes

Gus Goat   Andy Ant   feet

12

sit   book   look

Dom Dog

Pat Cat

Gus Goat

Andy Ant

Activity

1 Look. Say the names.
Write the letters. ⚫✏️

1  Dom Dog

2  at at

3  us oat

4  ndy nt

5  octor anda

Doctor Panda

Read the story

Pat Cat sees Dom Dog in his garden.

Dom Dog is not happy.
He is hot.

19

Dom Dog's head is hot.
Pat Cat has got Dom Dog's
hand.

Doctor Panda has big, black eyes. He has a blue bag.

23

Gus Goat helps Doctor Panda.

Dom Dog sits.
He looks at a book.

Dom Dog is in his garden.
He is happy. He is not hot.

Pat Cat, Gus Goat, and
Andy Ant are happy, too.

Activities

2 Color in words with the sound *ee* in green. Color in words with the sound *oo* in blue. Say the words. 📖 💬

look

book

teeth

feet

3 **Say the words. Match.** 🗣 📖

teeth

mouth

eyes

feet

book

hand

4 Look. Write the words. Say the words.

1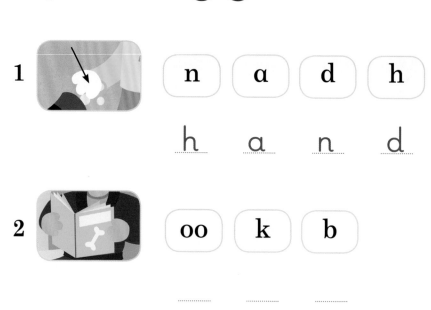

n   a   d   h

h   a   n   d

2

oo   k   b

....

3

b   g   a

....

4

ee   f   t

....

5 **Look. Say the words.**
Write the letters.

hand   happy   He   his   hot

1 Dom Dog is not h appy.

2 ____e is hot.

3 His ____and is hot, too.

4 He is very ____ot.

5 Doctor Panda is ____is doctor.

Starter Level A and B

The Zoo

978–0–241–28346–2

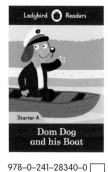

Dom Dog
and his Boat

978–0–241–28340–0

Ted in Bed

978–0–241–28342–4

The Fun Run

978–0–241–28343–1

Brother Blue

978–0–241–28338–7

Doctor Panda

978–0–241–28339–4

Farmer Carl

978–0–241–28341–7

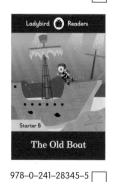

The Old Boat

978–0–241–28345–5